ASTRONAUT TO ZODIAC

ZODIAC A Young Stargazer's Alphabet

ROGER RESSMEYER

CROWN PUBLISHERS, INC. • New York

For Joe and Ruth,
who gave me a telescope
when I was nine

The author's special thanks go to Jain Ressmeyer, Jurrie
van der Woude, Mike Gentry, Isabel Warren-Lynch,
Tracy Halliday, and Simon Boughton.

Published by Crown Publishers, Inc., a Random
House company, 225 Park Avenue South, New
York, New York 10003. CROWN is a trademark
of Crown Publishers, Inc. Manufactured in
Japan.

Library of Congress Cataloging-in-Publication Data
Ressmeyer, Roger, 1954–
    Astronaut to zodiac : a young stargazer's
alphabet / Roger Ressmeyer. — 1st ed.
    Summary: Photographs and text of things
both astronomical and astronautical form an
alphabet book for the "stargazer."
    1. Astronomy—Dictionaries, Juvenile.
  2. Astronomy—Juvenile literature.
[1. Astronomy—Dictionaries.
  2. Astronautics—Dictionaries.
  3. Alphabet.] I. Title.
QB14.R47 1992
520'.3—dc20   92-9615
ISBN 0-517-58805-6 (trade)
       0-517-58806-4 (lib. bdg.)
10 9 8 7 6 5 4 3 2 1   First Edition

Astronauts are people who ride rockets into space. In space there is no air to breathe, and temperatures can range from super hot to freezing cold. A spacesuit contains air to breathe and keeps the astronaut's body at the right temperature. Since 1961, astronauts have explored space around the Earth and have landed on the surface of the Moon. In the future, they may travel to moons and planets that are even farther away. This new spacesuit is being tested for possible use outside NASA's planned space station.

AX-5 spacesuit.

A
Astronauts
wear spacesuits for protection.

Surrounding the Earth is a layer of life called the biosphere.

B

Earth from **Apollo 10,** 1969.

Our home is the third of nine planets orbiting the Sun. We call it Earth. Surrounding the Earth is a region where plants and animals live. This layer of life is called a biosphere. It reaches from deep in the ocean, where fish swim, to high in the sky, where birds fly. The other planets in the solar system don't have biospheres. Planets closer to the Sun are too hot, and planets farther away are too cold. Some have atmospheres made of poisonous gases. But on Earth, conditions are just right for life. From space, our biosphere looks thin and delicate, reminding us how fragile the Earth is. Pollution can damage the biosphere. It's up to all of us to keep our home planet clean.

Astronauts photographed these craters on the Moon's surface. They were formed billions of years ago. Large chunks of rock called "asteroids," and smaller rocks called "meteoroids," raced around the Sun faster than a speeding rocket. Crashing into the Moon, they exploded, making craters. Similar collisions left craters on most of the solar system's other planets and moons. If you look at the Moon through binoculars, you can see some of the bigger craters.

Craters of the Moon from **Apollo 10,** 1969.

Craters **cover the Moon's surface.**

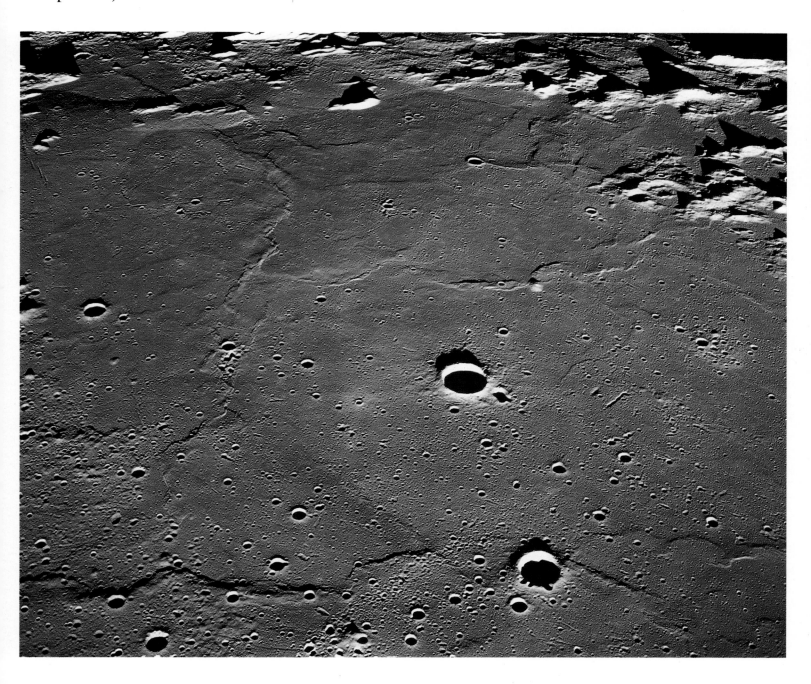

D

Comets grow dust tails as they approach the Sun.

Comets are big, dirty snowballs several miles across that orbit the Sun. They spend most of their time far away, near the outer limit of the solar system, but every few years a bright one zooms close to the Sun. As it approaches, the snowball gets hotter and begins to melt. A dust tail grows, formed from dust particles in the melting ice. The tail is millions of miles long and so thin that you can see stars through it. The most famous comet, Halley's Comet, returns to Earth's neighborhood every 76 years. The last time was in 1986.

Halley's Comet, 1986.

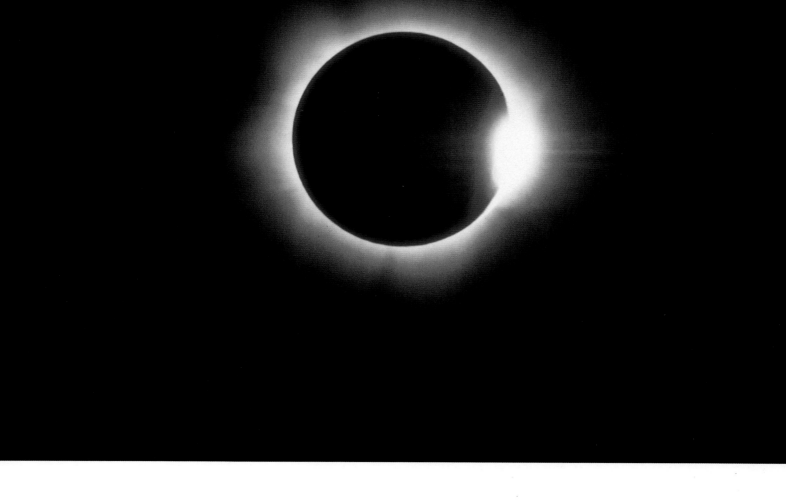

Diamond-ring effect at the end of a total eclipse, 1970.

When the Moon passes between the Earth and the Sun, an eclipse of the Sun takes place. The Moon seems to move in front of the Sun. At first, a black notch appears on the Sun's face. It grows bigger and bigger until the Sun is completely hidden behind the Moon's black disk. For a few minutes, the eclipse is total and the sky is dark. Then a bit of the Sun reappears on one side of the Moon. For a second or two, the eclipse looks like a diamond ring in the sky. The *only* time it is safe to look at the Sun is during the complete darkness of totality. Looking directly at the Sun at other times can cause blindness and is very dangerous. ►See *Umbra*

During an eclipse, the Sun is hidden behind the Moon.

E

F

There is a full Moon every 29½ days.

As the Moon orbits the Earth, it seems to change shape. Sometimes we see just a sliver. This is called a "crescent" Moon. Other times the Moon is oval, or "gibbous" (pronounced GIB-us). Once every 29½ days, we see a full Moon, which looks completely round. These different shapes are called "phases," and they appear because the Moon has no light of its own. Instead, it reflects the light of the Sun. The side facing the Sun is lit; the other side is in darkness. As the Moon orbits the Earth, the amount we see of the Moon's sunlit side changes. At full Moon we see all of the Moon's sunlit side. At a "new" Moon we cannot see the Moon at all because its sunlit side faces away from us. In between new and full Moons lie the other phases.

Full Moon over the Pacific Ocean.

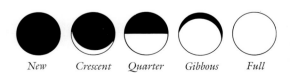

New Crescent Quarter Gibbous Full

Spiral galaxy.

A galaxy is a collection of billions of stars. The Sun and its nine planets belong to one such galaxy, which we call the Milky Way. Many galaxies, including our own, look like this one—a spinning wheel of stars in space. Astronomers call this a "spiral" galaxy. Other kinds of galaxies include "elliptical" galaxies, which are round or oval in shape, and "irregular" galaxies, which have no specific shape. The universe is made up of trillions of galaxies, each containing billions of stars. ▶See *Milky Way*

Many galaxies look like spinning wheels of stars.

Engineers build space habitats for astronauts to live in.

Space station **Freedom.**

A habitat is a place where animals and plants are able to live. Because there is no air in space, engineers build artificial habitats for astronauts to live in. The first space habitats were tiny little capsules barely big enough for one person. As larger rockets came along, two people, and then three, could fly together in space. Today's space shuttle holds seven astronauts. This photo shows a ground model of the biggest space habitat planned today, space station *Freedom*. Orbiting 200 miles above the Earth, *Freedom* could serve as a base for spaceships on their way to and from the Moon and planets.

One of the most unusual moons in the solar system is Io (pronounced EE-oh). Io orbits around the planet Jupiter. About the same size as Earth's moon, it looks like a giant pizza in space. Io was photographed by two robot space probes, *Voyager 1* and *Voyager 2,* in 1979. They discovered active volcanoes on Io. The volcanoes shoot hot sulfur into space. As the sulfur cools, it falls back onto Io's surface and covers it with a brightly colored crust. This photo shows a volcanic eruption shooting 200 miles above Io's rim.

Io, a moon of Jupiter.

Jupiter's moon Io looks like a pizza in space.

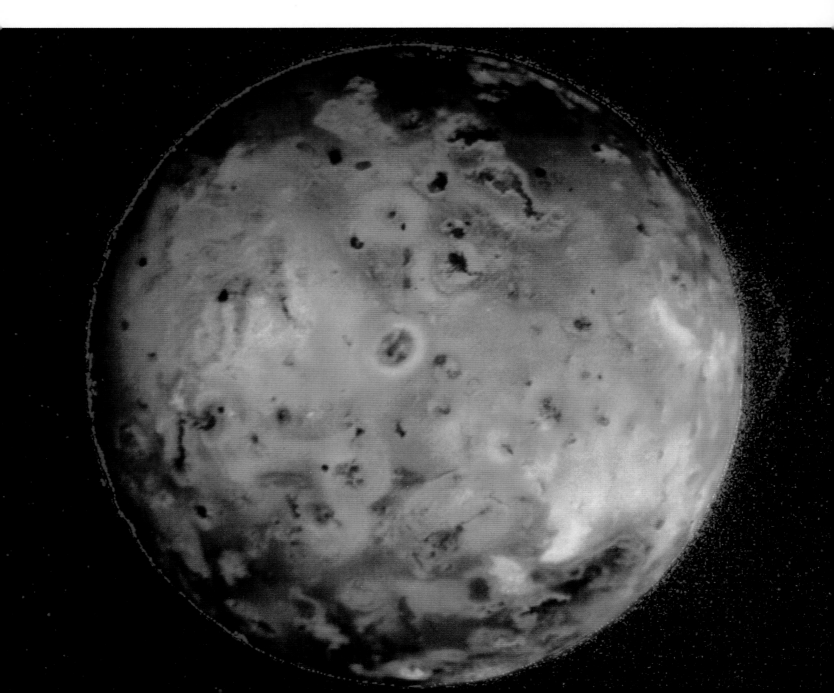

Beneath Jupiter's clouds there is no solid ground to stand on.

J

Planet Jupiter.

Jupiter is the biggest planet in the solar system. Its diameter is nearly 11 times that of the Earth. A kaleidoscope of clouds and storms swirls through Jupiter's atmosphere. The biggest of these is called the Great Red Spot. It has raged for hundreds of years and is big enough to swallow three whole Earths. Jupiter's atmosphere is mostly hydrogen gas. But beneath the clouds there is no solid ground to stand on. Instead, pressure turns the gas into a liquid, surrounding the planet in a bottomless ocean of liquid hydrogen. To the right of the Great Red Spot in this photograph is one of Jupiter's moons, Io.
►See *Planet*

The Kennedy Space Center, on the edge of the Atlantic Ocean in Florida, is where American rockets blast off for space. All NASA's manned spacecraft, from the first Mercury flights in 1961 to the Apollo moonshots and today's shuttle launches, have started here. When ready, rockets are loaded with fuel, and then astronauts climb aboard. Spectators gather. Launch control counts down, "...five, four, three, two, one—liftoff!" The ground shakes, and thousands of frightened birds take flight. The rocket climbs faster and faster until it is just a dot in the sky. At the Kennedy Space Center, work begins for the next launch.

Launch of shuttle **Discovery**, 1988.

K
Rockets are launched from the Kennedy Space Center.

Six lunar landings took place between 1969 and 1972.

L

Astronaut John Young jumping and saluting, **Apollo 16**, 1972.

The first manned lunar landing took place on July 20, 1969. After a three-day flight from Earth, astronauts Neil Armstrong and Buzz Aldrin touched down in a rocket-powered lunar lander called the *Eagle*. Astronaut Michael Collins waited overhead, circling the Moon in an Apollo spacecraft. Armstrong and Aldrin walked around for 2½ hours, collecting rocks and setting up experiments. Ten more astronauts landed on the Moon before the Apollo program ended. Some drove around in a special car called a lunar rover. In this picture, taken during the fifth Apollo landing, a rover is parked in front of the lander.

On a moonless night, far away from city lights, a silvery band of light can be seen stretching across the sky. Looking through binoculars, you realize that this band is actually the light from millions of distant stars. We call it the Milky Way, and it is part of the galaxy in which we live. The Milky Way Galaxy is a collection of stars and is shaped like a giant disk with spiral arms. The Sun and its planets are a little more than halfway out from the center, in one of the arms. When you look at the Milky Way in the night sky, you are looking at the disk edge-on. It is in this direction that the most stars lie—but in fact, all the stars you can see are part of the Milky Way Galaxy. This picture shows the center of the Milky Way straight overhead. ▶ See *Galaxy*

Milky Way in the sky over Chile.

The silvery band in the night sky is called the Milky Way.

Nebulae are where stars and planets are born.

N

The Great Nebula in the constellation Orion.

A nebula is a giant cloud of gas and dust in space. Some glow with light of their own or with light reflected from nearby stars. Others are dark clouds that show up as black patches in front of a starry background. Nebulae are where stars and planets are born. Slowly, the cloud of gas collapses. Over millions of years, the gases press more and more tightly together. As the pressure rises, the center of the cloud becomes super hot. With a blinding flash, nuclear reactions give birth to a new star. The nebula in this picture is 1,500 light-years from Earth and about 30 light-years across.

Telescopes are kept in observatories.

Modern telescopes are kept in observatories on high mountains far from city lights. With clear, dark skies, the telescopes see far into space. This observatory is almost three miles above the ocean, on top of a volcano in Hawaii. The observatory dome shields the telescope from wind and light. The curved star trails above the building are caused by the spinning of the Earth. As the Earth spins, the stars seem to travel through the sky. During one day, the stars appear to make complete circles around the Earth. This photo shows their movement during two hours. Because the camera was pointed at the North Star, above the Earth's North Pole, the stars trace circles around a stationary point.
► See *Telescope*

Observatory with star trails, Mauna Kea, Hawaii.

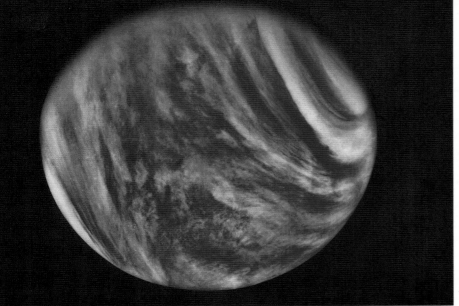

Venus

Mars

Saturn

Thousands of years ago, Greek sky watchers noticed bright dots of light moving very slowly among the stars. They named them "planets," which comes from the Greek word *planētēs,* meaning "wanderer." Today we know that the planets are ball-shaped worlds orbiting the Sun. There are nine known planets, of which Earth is the third. Venus is the brightest and nearest to us. It is about the same size as Earth and is covered with clouds. Mars is only half the size of Earth and has a cold, thin atmosphere and red dust everywhere. Saturn, sixth from the Sun, is a giant gas planet surrounded by beautiful rings. The rings are made of pieces of ice and rock ranging in size from tiny specks to boulders bigger than a house. The other five planets are Mercury, Jupiter, Uranus, Neptune, and Pluto. ►See *Jupiter*

Planet means "wanderer" in Greek.

P

First footprints on the Moon, **Apollo 11**, July 20, 1969.

When the first astronauts set foot on the Moon, it was a continuation of humanity's quest to explore the unknown. Since the beginning of history, people have built craft to carry them beyond the frontiers of the known world. Today's frontier is the solar system. Robot spacecraft have already visited distant planets. Someday, astronauts may follow. Our quest in space will probably result in permanent bases on the Moon, Mars, and beyond.

The first steps on the Moon were a part of humanity's quest in space.

Q

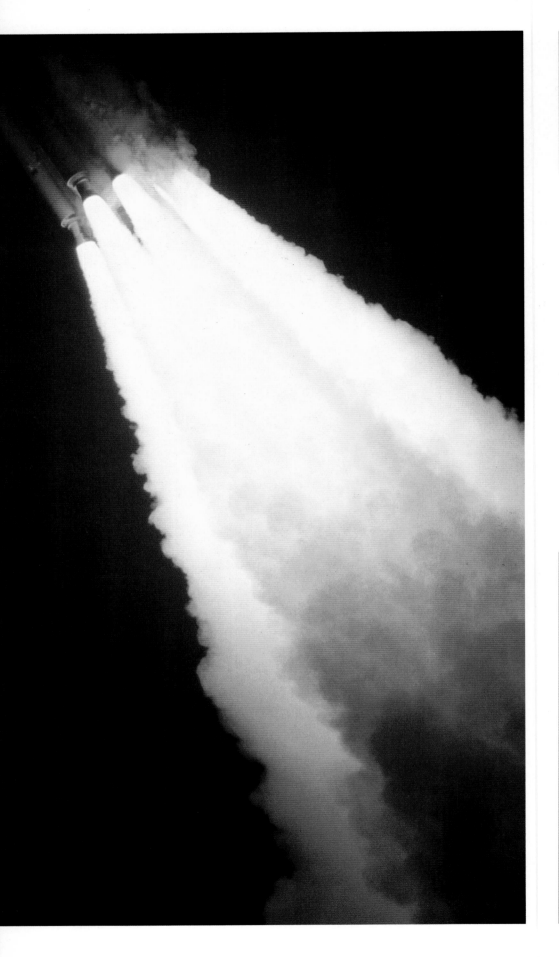

R

Rockets

carry spacecraft into space.

Rockets carry spacecraft off the Earth and into space. Rockets are powerful engines that move in one direction by shooting hot gases in the other—like an inflated balloon that flies around your room when you let go of it. To get into orbit around the Earth, a rocket must travel fast enough for its speed to balance the tug of the Earth's gravity. Any slower and gravity will pull it back to Earth. Any faster and it will escape the Earth's gravity altogether and travel off into space. The speed at which rockets go into orbit is about 17,000 miles per hour, or 30 times the speed of the average jet plane. This Japanese rocket has seven engines that all burn at the same time.

Japanese H-1 rocket launch, 1989.

A spacecraft is a vehicle that works in space. There are many kinds. Some, like the space shuttle, carry men and women into orbit. Others are complicated robots that are controlled from the ground. Robot spacecraft called satellites orbit the Earth, taking weather photographs, relaying telephone calls and television pictures, and performing many other jobs. Robots also travel beyond Earth's orbit to moons and planets, where they do experiments and take pictures so that we can learn more about distant worlds. This photograph shows a robot spacecraft called *Galileo*. *Galileo* was launched in 1989 on a mission to study the planet Jupiter and its moons.

Spacecraft **Galileo** during tests before launch.

The spacecraft *Galileo* was launched toward Jupiter in 1989.

S

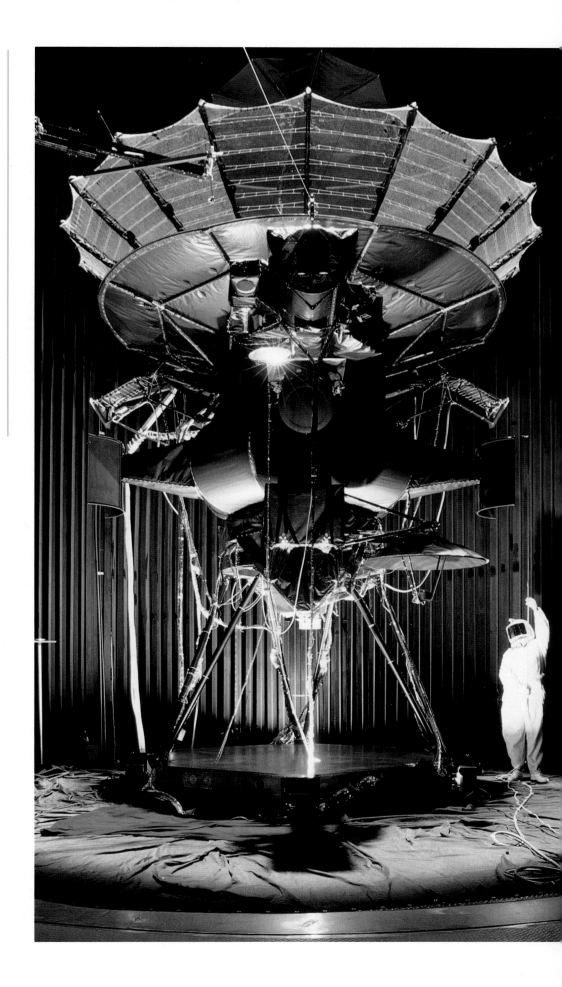

Keck telescope, Hawaii.

There are several kinds of telescopes. An optical telescope gathers and magnifies the light from stars and galaxies. The biggest optical telescope in the world is the Keck telescope. It uses a mirror 33 feet across to gather light. Another kind of telescope, the radio telescope, studies radio waves. This radio telescope is called the Very Large Array. It uses 27 dishes to collect radio waves from deep space. Many amateur stargazers keep small optical telescopes in their homes, and with them they make important discoveries, such as finding new comets. A small telescope like this one will show you the rings of Saturn, the craters on the Moon, and if you live away from the city, where the sky is dark, beautiful star clusters and distant galaxies.

▶See *Observatory*

Very Large Array, New Mexico.

Telescopes are used by astronomers to study the stars.

2.4-inch home telescope.

T

In our solar system, only the Sun makes its own light. One side of each planet and moon, the side that faces the Sun, is always lit up. We call that daylight. On the other side, facing away from the Sun, it is night. Every moon and planet casts a long, dark shadow into space. This dark shadow is called the umbra. The umbra is shaped like an ice cream cone. The moon or planet is the ball of ice cream at the top, and the shadow forms the cone. The cone's tip points away from the Sun. When the Earth passes through the Moon's umbra, we see an eclipse of the Sun. In this photo, taken at the end of a total eclipse, the edge of the Moon's round, black umbra stretches across the sky.
► See *Eclipse*

Moon's umbra, photographed from a jet plane.

The Moon's dark shadow is called its umbra.

V

Maat Mons is a five-mile-high volcano on the planet Venus.

Volcanoes are found on several of the solar system's planets and moons. They are holes in the crust through which molten rock, gas, and ash escape from the hot interior. As a volcano erupts, a high, cone-shaped mountain builds up around the hole. Earth has hundreds of active volcanoes. Maat Mons, the five-mile-high volcano in this picture, is on the planet Venus. Because the surface of Venus is always hidden by clouds, the picture was created using radar data collected by the spacecraft *Magellan,* which orbited overhead. A computer converted *Magellan*'s measurements of Venus's surface into a low-angle view of Maat Mons, and added color to the picture.

Maat Mons, volcano on Venus.

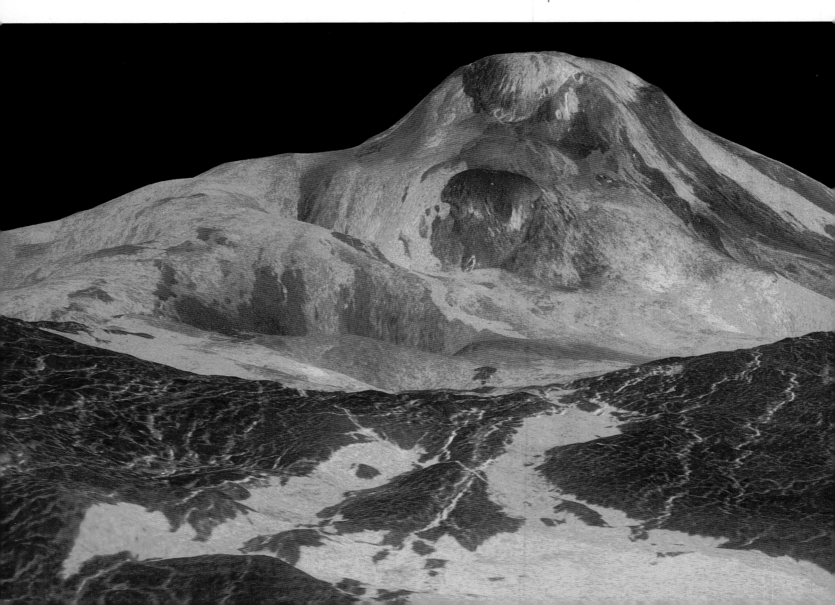

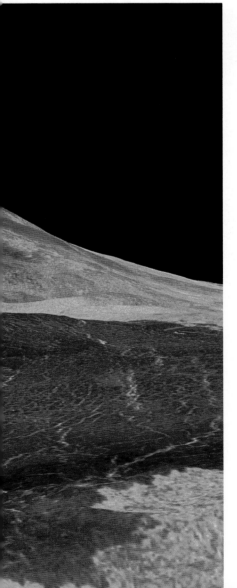

Ed White during the first U.S. walk in space.

In 1965, astronauts first left their spacecraft and learned how to walk in space. This picture shows U.S. astronaut Ed White floating outside his *Gemini* capsule. He wears a spacesuit filled with air. The visor on his helmet shields his eyes from dangerous radiation. To move around, he uses a little rocket, which he holds in his hand. A long cable, or "umbilical cord," connects him to the spacecraft. Without it, he could drift away.

The first walk in space was in 1965.

W

In addition to heat and light, the Sun gives off x-rays.

In addition to heat and light, stars give off other forms of energy such as x-rays. This picture of our Sun was taken with a special telescope that shows x-ray radiation. The bright patches and swirls show where the x-rays shoot into space. The Sun's atmosphere, or "corona," glows with x-ray energy. The x-rays are created deep inside the Sun by the same nuclear reactions that release heat and light. By studying x-rays, astronomers can learn more about conditions in the Sun.

X-ray picture of the Sun.

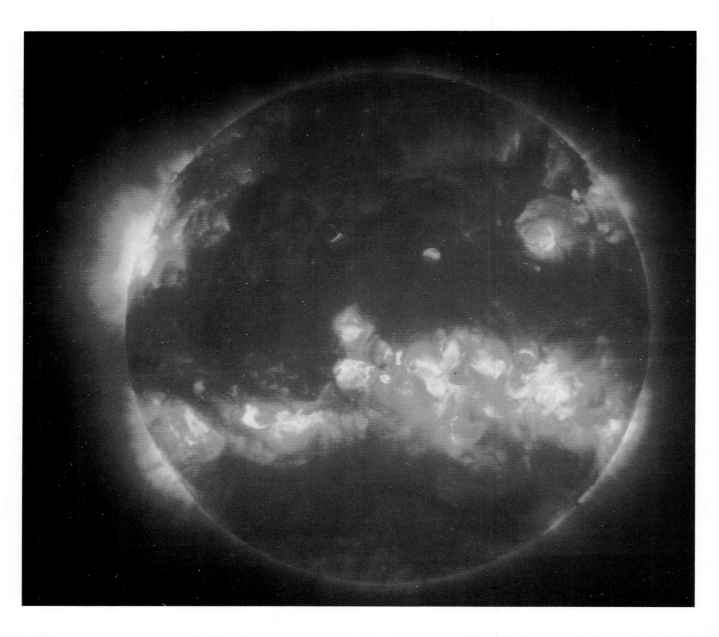

Stonehenge, England.

Many of the words we use to describe periods of time also describe the Earth's motion in space. A day is the amount of time it takes the Earth to spin once around on its own axis. A year is the amount of time—365¼ days—that it takes the Earth to make one complete orbit around the Sun. Four thousand years ago, people in England set up this circle of rocks, called Stonehenge, to measure the passage of time. One rock, called the "Heelstone," pointed toward sunrise on the "summer solstice," the longest day of the year. Other rocks marked the positions of sunrise and sunset during fall, winter, and spring.

A year is the amount of time Earth takes to go once around the Sun.

Y

Z During a year, the Sun travels through the *zodiac.*

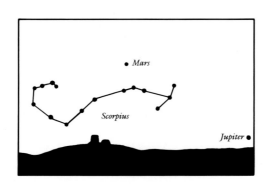

During the course of the year, the Sun's position among the stars appears to change. It traces a path through 12 constellations called the zodiac, or "circle of animals." They are Capricorn, the Goat; Aquarius, the Water Bearer; Pisces, the Fishes; Aries, the Ram; Taurus, the Bull; Gemini, the Twins; Cancer, the Crab; Leo, the Lion; Virgo, the Virgin; Libra, the Scales; Scorpius, the Scorpion; and Sagittarius, the Archer. In this picture, taken just after sunset, the Sun is in Libra. Scorpius is clearly visible, and in four weeks the Sun will have moved into Scorpius. The planets also move through the zodiac. Here, Jupiter, just above the sunset, is in Libra. Mars is in Scorpius.

Sunset at McDonald Observatory, Texas.

Glossary

Astronomy   The study of the stars, galaxies, planets, nebulae, and other objects in space. *Astronomers* are experts in the science of astronomy.

Atmosphere   The gases that surround a planet, moon, or star, and that are held in place by gravity. We call the Earth's atmospheric gases "air." Air is mostly nitrogen and oxygen.

Constellation   A pattern formed by groups of stars in the sky, most of which were first named by ancient astronomers. The 88 constellations are named after the animals, people, or objects that their shapes suggest.

Gravity   The force of attraction between objects in space. If you throw a ball into the air, the Earth's gravity causes it to fall back to the ground. Earth's gravity also keeps the Moon in orbit around the Earth; similarly, the Sun's gravity keeps the Earth in orbit around the Sun. The strength of an object's gravitational pull depends on its mass. The more massive the object, the greater its force of gravity.

Light-year   The distance that light travels in one year—about six trillion miles. Astronomers use light-years to measure the incredible distances between objects in space. For example, the nearest star to our solar system is over four light-years—about 26 trillion miles—away.

Moon   A natural satellite orbiting a larger planet. Some planets have dozens of moons; others have none.

NASA   National Aeronautics and Space Administration. The U.S. space agency, set up by Congress in 1958 to supervise U.S. space activities.

Orbit   The path of one object in space around another, heavier one. Moons orbit around planets; planets orbit around stars; and stars orbit around the center of galaxies.

Solar System   The Sun and all the planets, moons, asteroids, meteors, and comets that orbit around it.

Star   A round, gaseous object in space that glows with its own light, such as our Sun. Gravity compresses matter at the core of a star, creating high temperatures and causing nuclear reactions. These nuclear reactions cause the star to give off heat and light.

Universe   Everything that exists, including the solar system, all the stars, all the galaxies, and every bit of matter in all of space.

Exploring Space From Your Home

Stargazing can be an exciting hobby. With a set of star charts, you can learn to recognize the constellations and planets. Many newspapers give the dates of unusual events, such as meteor showers (when you can see dozens of shooting stars every hour) or lunar eclipses (when the full moon glows dim red).

Ordinary seven-power binoculars will show you Jupiter's moons, craters on the Moon, star clusters, and thousands of stars in the Milky Way. A small telescope will let you see more, including the rings of Saturn and dim nebulae and galaxies. Most cities and many towns have clubs for amateur astronomers. At "star parties" you can look through larger telescopes and learn more about the sky.

Your town or school library will have many books and magazines about space.

Sky and Telescope magazine is a great place to start. Many cities have planetariums and museums that teach about the constellations, space travel, and our place in the universe.

In some areas there are model-rocket clubs for those interested in space travel. Rocketeers build and fly small rockets as much as several thousand feet into the air. These detailed models return on parachutes or on wings like those of the space shuttle.

Almost every state has a special "space place" to visit, such as the Kennedy Space Center in Florida, the Palomar Mountain Observatory in California, the Hayden Planetarium in New York City, or the Air & Space Museum in Washington, D.C.

Have fun exploring the sky, and may your evenings of stargazing be dark and clear!